Book and Cover design by Boilerplate Books, LLC
ISBN: 978-1-7347934-5-1
Print Edition, 2023
10 9 8 7 6 5 4 3 2 1

For Janet (aka, Mimi,) Rían and Kaivan

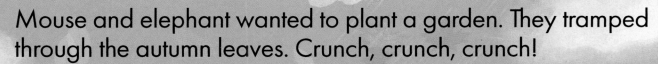

Mouse and elephant wanted to plant a garden. They tramped through the autumn leaves. Crunch, crunch, crunch!

They trekked through winter snow. Flump, flump, flump!
Until they found a perfect sunny spot.

Winter is when seed catalogs arrive in the mail.

Mouse and elephant decided to plant pumpkins.

Elephant placed an order
for pumpkin seeds.

They placed an "x" on the calendar and patiently waited and waited...

And waited.

Until a small box
arrived in the mail.

Pumpkin seeds!

It was too cold to plant them outside, so they placed seeds into small pots with a little soil...

and left those pots on sunny windowsills, where the seeds began to sprout.

It was time to prepare the garden.

Elephant dug up row after row of rich earth.
Mouse removed small rocks and weeds.

They planted each pumpkin one elephant foot apart.

Gave each a drink of water.

Under the warm sun and springtime rains the pumpkins grew and grew.

Mouse weeded the budding pumpkins with a little help from elephant.

Small pumpkins grew bigger and changed color from green to orange.

By early fall, the pumpkins were ripe.

Elephant picked a pumpkin...

and wandered off to
enjoy a pumpkin snack.

Mouse picked a pumpkin, but couldn't budge it.

Maybe if it was smaller.

Elephant returned to the sounds of nibbling.

It was mouse!

"This pumpkin is too heavy!" mouse complained.

If we work together, we can harvest all these pumpkins.

We can create a feast to share all winter.

Mouse found recipes for pumpkin muffins and pumpkin pie.

Working together they removed the sticky pumpkin pulp filled with seeds.

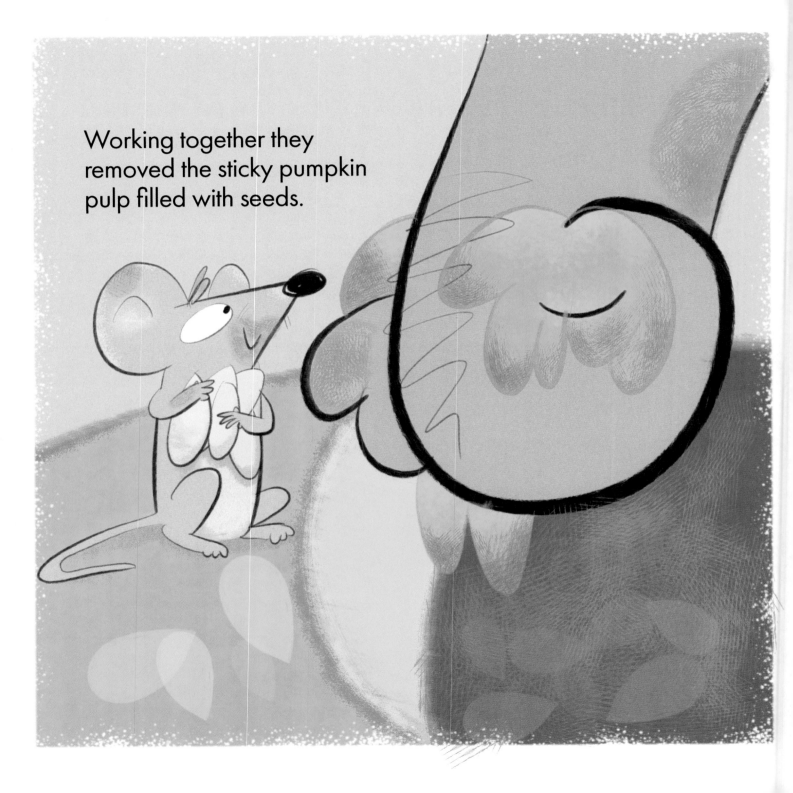

Each pumpkin had enough seeds to plant a whole new garden!

Mouse placed the seeds on a small paper towel to let them dry.

Then stored them
in a jar for next
year's garden.

They made pumpkin soup... and pumpkin bread...

and pumpkin pie... and pumpkin muffins with blueberries.

They ate and ate until they could eat no more.

The autumn rains and winter snows would soon arrive.
The garden enjoyed a well-deserved nap.

And so did mouse and elephant.

Ways to Explore this Book

LEARN more about elephants and their favorite food – pumpkins!

DRAW a picture of a pumpkin.

EXPLORE pumpkin recipes to make at home.

COUNT the seeds you find in fruits or vegetables.

GO OUTSIDE and explore the plants you find growing around you.

LOOK UP what plants need to grow.

TELL a story about you and your best friend.

TALK about a time when you had to wait for something.

Welcome to the neighborhood!

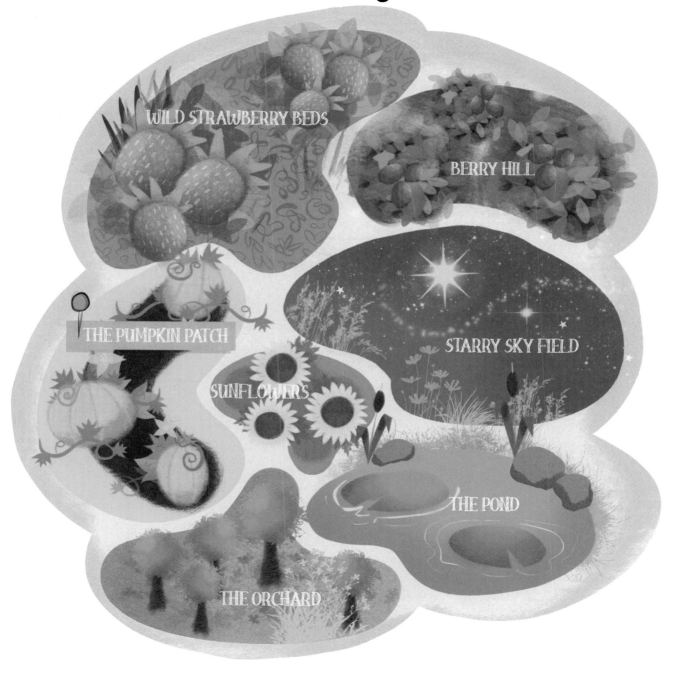

Made in the USA
Middletown, DE
24 June 2023

33483666R00029